THE WRONG BOOK

THE WRONG BOOK

WRITTEN BY **Drew Daywalt**

ILLUSTRATED BY **Alex Willmore**

PHILOMEL

PHILOMEL

An imprint of Penguin Random House LLC, New York

First published in the United States of America by Philomel,
an imprint of Penguin Random House LLC, 2024

Text copyright © 2024 by Drew Daywalt
Illustrations copyright © 2024 by Alex Willmore

Philomel is a registered trademark of Penguin Random House LLC.
The Penguin colophon is a registered trademark of Penguin Books Limited.

Visit us online at PenguinRandomHouse.com.

Library of Congress Cataloging-in-Publication Data is available.

ISBN 9780593621967

3 5 7 9 10 8 6 4 2

Manufactured in China

TOPL

Edited by Jill Santopolo
Design by Opal Roengchai
Text set in Futura LT Pro and Kabouter

The illustrations were created in pencil, ink, and Photoshop.

To Austin and Alex —D. D.

For Dara and Walter —A. W.

And apples go

CRUNCH
CRUNCH
CRUNCH!

when you eat them!

Yummy!
What's next?

This is a flower.

Flowers grow all over the world and come in many pretty colors. They often smell wonderful.

Mmmm, they sure do!

And flowers go

CHUGGA
CHUGGA
CHOOOO
CHOOOO!!!!

Wait, what?

And here is a bicycle.

The bicycle says

BURRRRP!

HUH?!

And here we see a great example of an elephant.
The elephant says

This is a firefighter.

And a firefighter says stuff like
"Hey! Let's go put out that fire!"

Okay.
That's better.

Yes. Yes.
Also good.
Keep going.

This is a lion.
Lions live on farms and say

Seriously?! Oh my gosh, NO!
That's a bicycle, and it lives in
the garage, or under your butt
when you ride it.

And it does NOT
say MOOOO!

You're right.
It doesn't say moo.

It says

COCK-A-DOODLE-DOOO!!!

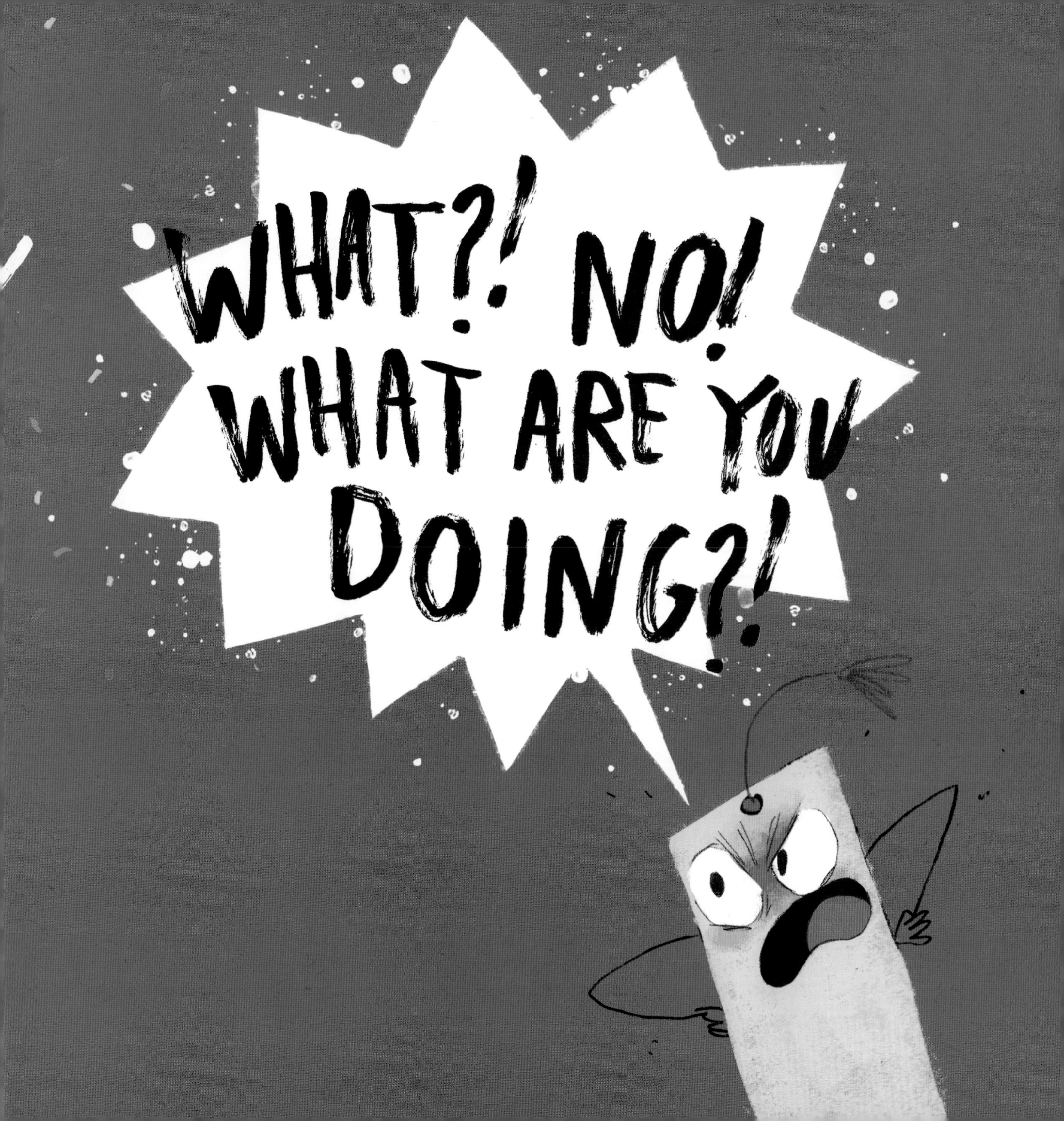
WHAT?! NO! WHAT ARE YOU DOING?!

This is a fish.
The fish says

Here is a yummy hamburger.
You can eat the yummy hamburger.
The hamburger says
BAWK BAWK
BAWK and COCK-A-DOODLE-DOOO!

Well, I guess if you can't beat 'em, join 'em!
PEW PEW PEW!
TWEET TWEET!

THE END!